Disney's
POCAHONTAS

THE
VOICE of the WIND

By Justine Korman
Illustrated by Peter Emslie and Don Williams

A GOLDEN BOOK • NEW YORK

Western Publishing Company, Inc., Racine, Wisconsin 53404

A soft breeze tickled the new green leaves, and white and yellow crocuses bloomed in the meadows. Spring had come at last! Every hand in the village was set to planting. From morning until late afternoon, Pocahontas planted seeds in the dark soil.

As always, Flit the hummingbird and Meeko the raccoon stayed close to their pretty young friend.

At the end of one long corn row, Pocahontas sighed. She enjoyed planting, but the spring breeze stirred a sweet restlessness in her heart.

"Wouldn't you love to find out what's beyond the bend in the river?" Pocahontas asked her masked friend.

Meeko shrugged. He was more interested in finding a way to eat some of the dried corn seed without Flit catching him.

As for Flit, he thought Pocahontas should stay safely near the village. He didn't care what was beyond the river bend.

"Well, I have to find out!" Pocahontas declared.

So that afternoon, as all the other villagers returned to their homes, Pocahontas slipped off on her own and paddled her canoe up the river.

Flit hummed around Pocahontas's head. He pointed his long beak toward Grandmother Willow's grove. He hoped the wise old tree spirit would talk some sense into Pocahontas.

But the young woman shook her head. "No, Flit. We're not going to visit Grandmother Willow. Today I want to discover some place I have never explored before."

Pocahontas stopped paddling for a moment and
Meeko jumped from the canoe to the riverbank to chase
grasshoppers. Then he played leapfrog with the frogs.
He waved his paws at Pocahontas.

"No, Meeko," she said. "I can't stop to play today.
Come along now, unless you'd rather stay behind."

Meeko climbed back into the canoe. But he hopped out again
at a strawberry patch.

Pocahontas left the canoe to pick some of the sweet berries, too.
They were delicious. But she still felt restless. "Come on, Meeko,"
she said. "Let's head for that bend in the river and new places
to explore."

Clouds began to gather in the blue sky. Branches swayed above
their heads. As it ruffled Pocahontas's hair, the wind whispered a
warning. But Pocahontas did not want to listen. Instead, she hurried
back to her canoe and paddled farther up the river.

With a sudden crack of thunder, rain poured from the sky. "Oh, not another spring shower!" Pocahontas exclaimed.

Then she noticed a cave on the riverbank. "We can take shelter there until the rain stops," Pocahontas said to her friends as she paddled to shore.

Flit flew anxiously around the mouth of the cave. He did not want to go inside. Pocahontas tugged her hair free of the bird's beak. "Stop being silly, Flit," she scolded. "It's just a cave."

Meeko hesitated at the dark entrance.

"Are you afraid, too?" Pocahontas asked him, shaking her head.

Pocahontas marched boldly into the cave. "At least it's dry
in here," she said, shaking the rainwater from her long hair. "We
can build a fire," she added, gathering some sticks.

Just then a low growl rumbled from the back of the cave. Meeko
hid behind Pocahontas. Flit flew up to the ceiling.

Pocahontas stood still, listening. Goose bumps tickled her damp
arms. "What was that?" she whispered.

A huge black bear stepped out of the shadows. It was waking late from its winter nap—and it wasn't at all happy to be disturbed!

Flit flew around the bear's head, hoping to distract it so Pocahontas could run away. But the beast just growled at the tiny bird.

Meeko offered the bear some strawberries. He thought the
sweet berries would keep the bear busy while Pocahontas
tiptoed out of the cave. But the berries were gone in seconds—
and the bear was still mad!

Pocahontas's mind raced. "What can I do?" she wondered. She thought of her friends and of wise old Grandmother Willow. And that gave her an idea! Wasn't Grandmother Willow always telling her to "listen to the wind"?

So Pocahontas listened. At first all she heard was the WHOOSH of the storm. But soon she heard the wind's own wild song. She started to sing along.

Pocahontas sang of springtime, of the sun, of the wind, of the new green leaves. She sang of the river winding between the mossy banks. She sang of the seeds in the dark earth drinking the rain.

Flit hummed along and Meeko drummed on some stones.
The bear stopped and listened. Soon he lowered his paws and
sank to the floor. His sleepy head dropped onto his furry chest.

Before long, the big bear was fast asleep.

Pocahontas put a finger to her lips. Meeko and Flit understood her at once. They followed her silently out of the cave.

"It's stopped raining," Pocahontas said, once they were outside.
The last rays of the setting sun glimmered on the river.
Raindrops sparkled on the new leaves.
The spring peepers sang their froggy song and the birds and
crickets chimed in.

"How could I have felt so restless with all of this around me?" Pocahontas asked her friends. Then she laughed. "I didn't need to find a faraway place to explore. I just needed to open my eyes a bit wider and to stop and listen to the music of the wind!"

Then Pocahontas and Meeko climbed into the canoe. And with Flit leading the way, they set out happily for home.